Zozo Afro

The boy who is very proud of his afro hair

Zozo Afro

*The boy who is very proud
of his afro hair*

Chuze Baba

Illustrated by Julia Pelikhovich

ISBN 978-2-9602222-0-3

Published by Chuze Baba

BL. Louis Mettewie Brussels, 1080, Belgium

32471271436

chuzeebaba@gmail.com

Illustrated by Julia Pelikhovich

Edited by Rosalind Scott

Cover design' by Michael Astatke

This book is dedicated to my son Eliam

6

Zozo was so excited about his 'Show and Tell' presentation for Mr Kono's class. He had been planning his presentation for that class for a long time.

He was standing in front of the mirror combing his big Afro hair, when his mother Keni walked into his room.

'So Zozo, did you finally decide what to take for your 'Show and Tell' presentation?' She asked.

'Mum, it's Zozo Afro. Please call me Zozo Afro. And I have decided to show my African Afro hair for the presentation.'

'Oh, ok. What are you going to say about your African Afro hair Zozo Afro?' Asked Keni.

'Well Mum, why don't you come and listen to my presentation, and find out?' Replied Zozo Afro. 'Mr Kono said we can invite anyone we like.'

'I would love too.' Said Mum.

Zozo Afro told his mum what time his presentation would be and left for school.

8

Mr Kono's class was at 10:00. Everyone was excited to do their Show and Tell. Zozo Afro looked around at his classmates; most of them had brought their favorite toys to show. His presentation was going to be quite different, but he wasn't worried.

Zozo Afro's presentation was right after his best friend Nunu's. Nunu had brought in a wooden toy car he made himself. When he had finished presenting, everyone including some parents who had come to watch, applauded him. Mr Kono was also impressed.

'Great job, Nunu.' He said. 'Ok, up next we have Zozo. Are you ready?'

'Yes, Mr Kono.' Said Zozo Afro, and he got up from his seat. He took one step forward and stopped. He had forgotten the most important thing! He checked in his backpack and took something out. Everyone was eager to see what he was getting out of his bag.

Zozo Afro took out a big, wooden comb. All of his classmates
laughed looking at the comb; what was he going to do with it?
'Please, everyone behave.' Said Mr Kono. 'Let's
see what Zozo has brought.'
Zozo Afro looked at his mother. She looked very proud
of him already. She gave him a look that said, 'You
can do it' and nodded her head.
Afro Zozo then stuck the big wooden comb in
his Afro hair and faced everyone.

Some students giggled, looking at him with the comb sticking out of his head.

'Ok Zozo, what did you bring today?' Asked Mr Kono.

'Today my presentation will be about my African Afro hair and this special comb.' Said Zozo Afro proudly.

He took the big comb out of his hair and started to comb his Afro while walking around the class. His classmates couldn't help but laugh.

Again Mr Kono warned them to keep quiet and listen to what Zozo had to say.

'I am Zozo Afro. And I am very proud of my African Afro hair.' Said Zozo Afro, walking around the room. Many of the students turned around in their seats so they could see him and his Afro hair.

'I love everything about my hair.' He said. 'I love that it's always in good shape. I love that it's dark. I love that it's unique. I love that it's stylish, and I love that if something falls and hits my head, it will protect me.'

Everyone laughed, including Mr Kono this time.

Zozo Afro continued, 'And, of course, it's the reason I'm so good-looking.'

Mr Kono started to applaud and everyone joined in.

Zozo Afro looked at his mum. She looked as if she couldn't be prouder. She was smiling at him and clapping at the same time.

'Ok, Zozo Afro. Is there anything you would like to tell us about your big comb?' Said Mr Kono.

'Of course,' Said Zozo Afro, excitedly. 'I got this nice comb from my grandfather. When he gave it to me, he told me to feel proud every time I use it. It's made of wood and his grandfather gave it to him too. That's my great-great grandfather. This comb is very old but still strong. And my grandpa told me a story about how this comb saved his grandfather's life. May I tell the story Mr Kono?' Asked Zozo Afro.

'Of course, Zozo Afro. I am sure everyone would love to hear your story.' Said Mr Kono, and he looked round at his students.

Everyone said, 'Yes, please tell us, Zozo Afro.'

Zozo Afro continued: 'A long time ago, my great-great grandfather and his friends went out hunting. While they were waiting for an antelope to show up, they were surprised by another animal: a Lion!

18

'They were all terrified. One of my great-great grandfather's friends ran away, but my great-great grandfather and his other two friends stayed calm. The lion came closer to them and roared.

'And then it got worse! Other family members of the lion showed up. They had smelled the men, and heard the first lion's roar, and planned to eat my great-great grandfather!

'One of my great-great grandfather's friends started saying his prayers. The other one froze to the spot, too afraid to move.

'But my great great grandfather was a brave man and no one could ever see when he was afraid. As the lions circled them, he got up to fight against the lions.

'When his friends saw his bravery, they both got up to help too, and held the lions off for as long as they could.

They tried to protect themselves with their spears, but the lions kept closing in. Then, one of the biggest lions grabbed my great great grandfather's spear in his teeth and threw it aside. He was empty handed. His friends fought as hard as they could to protect him and themselves, but the lions were very strong.'

Everyone was listening with excitement. All eyes were on Zozo Afro. He continued: 'As my great-great grandfather was looking around for something to protect himself from the lions, he remembered the comb that he always carried with him.

'You see, my great-great grandfather had Afro hair, just like me. And he was carrying the comb in his beautiful Afro hair, just like me right now.' Afro Zozo demonstrated how he could put the comb in his Afro hair, and it would stay put.

'My great-great grandfather took this wooden comb out of of his hair and turned to face the biggest lion. He gave him a fierce look and held this comb right up, roaring like the lion had. 'Rooooooaaaaaar!'

Zozo Afro, roared like a lion, holding his comb up to show the class how his great-great grandfather had faced down the biggest lion. The whole class was listening with their eyes wide open, as if they were watching the real scene.

'My great-great grandfather roared and stared at the lion with his fierce eyes and stood as tall as he could with his African Afro hair and held up this wooden comb. And that big lion, who was the leader of the group, turned and ran for his life.

'All the rest of the lions followed. My great-great grandfather's two friends couldn't believe their eyes, but he just kept on roaring until all the lions were out of sight.

'The three brave men kissed this wooden comb, because it had saved their lives. And after that day my great-great grandfather was always known as 'The Brave Afro with the Comb'. And all the men in their neighborhood started to grow Afro hair and put a wooden comb in it everywhere they went.'

Zozo Afro paused for a moment and looked around at his classmates.

'That's the story of my wooden comb.' He said. 'And I am so proud of my African Afro hair every time I use it. Thank you.'

Everyone got up from their seats to applaud Zozo Afro. He could hardly believe what he was seeing. When he looked at his mum, she was fighting back her tears.

Mr Kono finally spoke. 'Oh, Zozo Afro, that was such a wonderful story. Thank you so much for sharing. You taught us a big lesson today. We should always be proud of how we are and love our looks.'

He looked around at the class and added, 'We are all beautiful as we are; we don't have to change anything. Look at Zozo Afro, he looks so great with his African Afro hair. And yes, your great-great grandfather was such a brave man, and I bet he would be so proud of you, Zozo Afro.'

Everyone applauded Zozo Afro again as he went back to his seat. All his classmates asked him if they could touch the historic wooden comb.

Zozo Afro was hero of the day.

Since then, Zozo Afro has continued to take care of his African Afro hair and his comb. He knows that one day he will give the comb to his grandson, and tell him the story of his great-great-great-great grandfather, and how he faced down a lion, using only his African Afro hair, and a wooden comb.

The End

Printed in Great Britain
by Amazon

42333308R00017